The Voice of the Dark World

Book and Necklace
Book 1

Taylor Wilson

CONTENTS

ACKNOWLEDGMENTS
Thank you to all my supporters. To those who
support me no matter what happens in my or
their life. To those who are able to hear voices
of other worlds.

PROLOGUE

Nothing will ever be the same again. Lacey looked around at the empty house: the dark corner in the living room that housed her mother's favorite armchair, the pile of dishes that she didn't have the heart to do, and most of all, the memories that lurked in every inch of the house that seemed so empty without Mom. A warm hand rubbed her back, and she turned to her father, attempting to smile. The smile came across as a grimace and her icy blue eyes filled with tears.

Her father pulled her close as silent tears ran down his own face.

Sobs wracked Lacey's throat and her

slender body shook with the thought that she would never see her mother again. "I can't believe she's gone." She whispered.

Her father patted her back. "Me neither." His eyes became glazed, far off, as if he was thinking of something that he could not verbalize.

It was funny what the mind remembered when going through the motions of normalcy. The funeral had been a sea of faces saying the same words again and again; "Our condolences." Her mother's death had been sudden and abrupt, slamming the brakes in their lives. Now, she could only think of how quickly the past two days had been and how much had changed in such a little amount of time.

Lacey's father hugged her again, holding tight to the only person left in his family. "Now we have to look out for each other, Lacey."

Lacey nodded silently in his embrace.

"And I'm here for you, no matter what you need. I know I cannot replace your mom, but I will do my best to fill that void."

Fresh tears left Lacey's eyes. "I'm lucky to have you, dad." Her words were hoarse and rough.

Suddenly, William released Lacey and opened his mouth as if to say something, but then closed it. He opened it again and Lacey could not help but think of him as a fish.

"What is it?" She asked.

William took a deep breath, collecting his thoughts. "Come with me, Lacey."

Puzzled, she followed him through the house to his office located in the back, near the kitchen; a small, ten-by-ten room meant to be a den. A single leather couch sat in one corner, facing the oak study table with a hutch filled to the brim with language books. As a child, Lacey would complain that none of his books had any pictures; "except for boring pictures of letters and runes!" she would often say. William would explain that those were the books he assigned his language arts students at University of Toronto and that they liked the pictures of runes. During these little tirades, Lacey's mother would just watch with a serene smile on her face, before scooping Lacey in her arms and planting a kiss atop her pigtailed head.

Lacey shook her head of the memory and sat down across the desk from her father. Today, just like always, the language books were nearly spilling out of the hutch, but now Lacey knew better than to take them for granted. Now she understood that they contained a world of knowledge she hoped her father would share with her one day.

The study smelled of parchment and ink, with a faint, flowery scent that ghosted over her from the pot of tulips on the windowsill. The flowers were nearly wilting now.

William leaned down to the bottommost drawer of his desk and pulled out a bundle of cloth. It made a dull thud as he put it down on the dark oak. For a while, he stared at the bundle, as if expecting it to combust or something.

Lacey cleared her throat.

William nodded, and then reached for the piece of twine that kept the cloth together. Lacey watched as he unwrap the bundle to reveal a large book, and a crudely wrapped, lumpy object. She sent a look to her dad before asking, "What's this?"

"Listen carefully, Lacey. This is something I have not told you, but crucial in finding out whom you are."

Lacey tilted her head questioningly; finding out who I am? She nearly laughed at the statement, not understanding why her father would say such a thing. However, when she looked at her father's serious, pursed-lipped expression, she understood that he is dead serious. "What do you mean, Dad?"

He pushed the book toward her, watching her expectantly.

The volume was thick, bound in black leather. It was old, but in excellent condition. She opened the heavy, cool, cover to find yellowing pages that seemed to be quite thicker than regular paper. She looked up with a narrowed eye to find her father watching her with an unreadable expression. She turned back to the book and flipped a few more pages. The words at first appeared written in English, with familiar letters. However, there was something strange. The words were barely readable, but at the same time familiar, as if someone had written a book using only anagrams. Sprinkled throughout the sentences were some symbols that were completely unfamiliar.

She looked up, confused. "Is this a new book for your class, Dad?"

He shook his head as a look of

disappointment passed over him. "There is also this." He reached inside the lumpy package, emitting a clinking noise as he pulled out a piece of jewelry so enchanting, the first thought that popped inside Lacey's head is 'are these real gems?'

William blew some dust over the stones and they shimmered in the afternoon sunlight. "Does this look familiar to you?" He asked as he extended the necklace for Lacey to take.

Brows furrowed, she took the necklace from his warm fingers and inspected it. Embedded inside pale gold were what appeared to be diamonds and emeralds. It was heavier than it looked, nearly causing her to drop it when she picked it off the oak desk. "Should it be familiar to me?" she asked.

William dropped his head. "No, I guess not." He sighed, "I just thought it was worth a shot."

Lacey gently placed the necklace back atop the paper it had come in. "No offence,

Dad, but why are you showing me these things? Especially when all I want to do is to go and sleep the day off?"

"It is time you learned the truth, Lacey." He gave his daughter such a serious look that she was stunned into silence.

She laid her hands on the table and met her father's eyes, then nodded slowly.

William took a deep breath, and his expression softened. "You're adopted, Lacey."

Her breath hitched. At first, she barely comprehended. "Adopted?" Her echo was low.

William nodded. "Yes, adopted. But not in the traditional way. Your mom and I found you as a baby seventeen years ago. We were walking in High Park, and your mom noticed a little basket by the lake. No one else seemed to notice it or give it much attention, but you know your curious mother." He smiled sadly.

Lacey nodded and smirked. Her mother had always been on the lookout for the most obscure facts and would often bring them up randomly.

William continued. "Well, when we inspected the basket, we were shocked to find a tiny baby, no older than six months, inside. I remember looking around frantically, but it seemed that you had been abandoned there." His ice blue eyes, so similar to Lacey's, welled up and he dabbed at them with a handkerchief. "I wanted to call the police, but your mother insisted that we take you home first."

Lacey's lips parted in disbelief. "But you never called the police, did you?"

William hung his head. "We did, a few days later. When no one decided to claim you, we adopted you." He took a long, shaky breath.

Lacey understood that this was a difficult topic for him. She herself was in shock to learn this, and momentarily entertained the idea that her father was just pulling her leg.

William continued, "After many unsuccessful attempts at having a child, we felt as if you had just fallen into our laps." He smiled his gaze far off as if reliving the memories. Then he shook his head and looked at the language book and necklace. "But you weren't alone at the bench that day." He pushed the items towards Lacey. "These were in the basket with you and they belong to you."

Lacey stared at the alien items. 'What am I supposed to do with these?' she thought. "I don't know what to do with them, Da" She paused. Should she still have called him her dad?

"To be honest, I was hoping that you would somehow recognize them." He hung his head again. "Silly of me, I know"

Lacey reached across the desk toward his hand. "It isn't silly, Dad." 'Yes, I should still call him dad,' she thought to herself. 'After all, he had been the one to raise her all of these years. The fact that she was adopted didn't change that.'

"But I have no idea what these are for, dad. It's just an old book and a necklace."

William nodded. "It may be an old book, but it is quite special."

Lacey tilted her head.

"The language in there isn't any that I've ever seen. Many languages have the same letters as English, but I can't decipher this. At first, the book was exciting to me, a linguistics student." He laughed. "Can you imagine? I was sure I had found my thesis goldmine!"

Lacey didn't respond.

He cleared his throat. "Well, I spent nearly all of my time trying to decipher the words but was unsuccessful every time."

"And the necklace?" Lacey asked, eyeing the object curiously.

"Your mom was the one to test that one out. At first, she would only wear it around the house, admiring the diamond and emerald stones."

Lacey smiled. The necklace was quite enchanting in its beauty.

William's face darkened. "But after a while, something was wrong."

"How so?"

'Did it break?' Lacey wondered.

"Your mother began to change. Her mannerisms became how I put this, meaner. She wasn't herself. Then things around her began to move of their accord."

Lacey's eyes widened. She shifted her black hair away from her face and leaned in on the desk, hanging on to every word her father said. She could react later, when he was finished and she was alone with her thoughts.

He nodded. "We thought the necklace was cursed and put it away until now." He took a deep breath, suddenly tired from revealing buried information. "I realize that this is a lot, Lacey, but I also stand by whatever you wish to do with this information."

Lacey gazed at the two items for what seemed like a long time. 'These must be very important if someone left them with me.' Perhaps if she took the time to understand the language in the book, could she ever decipher it? Would it possibly lead to her finding her birth parents? Did she even want to find them? A dull throb began to pulsate in her temples, the start of a migraine. With a deep breath she said, "I need some time to think." She took the book and necklace and stood up to leave.

"Lacey?" Her father called before she exited the room.

She turned to face him, attempting a

neutral expression.

"I love you no matter what." His ice blue eyes were wide and sincere.

She nodded. "I love you too, Dad." She closed the door softly behind her.

Each step on the staircase was heavier due to the items in her hands. She opened the door to her bedroom and was instantly hit with the scent of air freshener Japanese Cherry Blossom, clipped on the wall. She flipped off the scent as her migraine intensified. A day in bed seemed inviting, but she knew sleep would not come so easily. She shoved the book and necklace in the far corner of her closet and climbed into bed to stew in the bombshell that had been dropped on her.

CHAPTER ONE

The dream trickled from Lacey's mind as a waterfall carries water down to the bottom, turned into white foam upon the rocks. She tried to remember the face she saw, but the more she concentrated, the more it disappeared. She kept her eyes closed in a futile attempt at recalling the picture, but it had already slipped far away into the deep recesses of her mind, only to be remembered when she dreamed of it again.

She sat up and pushed down the purple comforter, part of a set that included frilly lilac pillows and silk sheets. Her feet slipped into fluffy house slippers and she heaved herself off the bed. The migraine of the previous day was now just the dull throb of the aftershock. Suddenly the trigger behind the headache returned to her like a speeding train. I'm adopted! The word felt foreign, unfamiliar in her mind. Then she remembered the two objects and rushed over to her closet to pull them out.

She ran a hand along the smooth and cool leather-bound cover, and then held up the necklace. Something about the jewels compelled her to open the clasp and hold it up to her neck, it felt warn and alive. Then she remembered her father's warning about it being cursed. She wasn't sure if she believed in that stuff but she put it back in the crepe paper just in case. She pushed the objects back to where they were and got up from the carpeted floor.

She walked over to the window and drew the curtains, narrowing her eyes when a burst of sunlight entered her room. Along the far wall was a white sleigh bed topped with lilac covers. She went over and made the bed.

Next to it were mirrored side tables with modern white lamps. The vanity table across the room beckoned her as she sees herself in the mirror.

Long black hair was messy due to sleep, and her ice blue eyes were puffy from crying so much. Her cheeks were slightly swollen, and she had dark circles under her eyes. With a sigh, she picked up her hairbrush and dragged it through the strands that had become too oily for her liking. For now, she simply took elastic and tied her hair at the nape of her neck. One hand reached for her makeup bag, but she stops. Did she really need that stuff at home? Maybe when she was seeing people.

She didn't bother to change her clothes and walked out of her room. From the stairs, she could hear her father shuffling around in the kitchen. She heard the clink-clink of dishes as she reached the bottom of the stairs. She saw her father alone in the kitchen her heart felt the heavy pain again. She immediately went over to the stove to help.

"Morning, Dad." Her voice was tinged with both their own pains and her love for her father

"Good morning, sweetheart." He planted a kiss atop her head as he handed her a plate of scrambled eggs and turkey bacon.

She set her plate on the round white table in front of the bay window, and then went to pour two mugs of coffee. She'd developed a taste for black coffee two years ago and has not been able to stop.

William smiled in a constrained way as he sat with his daughter. The absent chair on the breakfast table was a heavy presence and neither father nor daughter let their gaze travel there. "Did you sleep okay?" He asked quickly.

Lacey nodded, although her night was filled with dreams that kept waking her.

For a while, there was only the clinking of cutlery on ceramic as the two ate their breakfast in silence. Lacey took a sip of coffee, letting the sweetness coat her mouth before swallowing. As a child, she never understood how adults could drink such a beverage, at least on purpose. She was still technically a child, but she felt as if she was much older today than she was a couple of days ago. She picked at the eggs, suddenly not hungry.

"I'm sorry you had to find out this way. Your mom and I wanted to tell you together, but well…" He trailed off with a far-away look in his eyes.

Lacey sighed. It is not his fault that she was abandoned as a baby, and she did not wish for him to feel sorry for that. But the right words didn't come and she closed her mouth.

William reached across the table, and she took his hand.

"Just know that I love you, and I will always be your father."

She sent him a genuine, sad smile and he took a deep breath before returning the gesture. They finished the rest of their meal in comfortable silence.

After breakfast, the doorbell rang.

"I'll get it." Lacey said behind her back as she left her father washing the dishes.

As soon as Lacey opened the door, a person who smelled strongly of fruity body spray and had a soft, fluffy sweater on swept her up into a tight hug.

"Hi, Sara," Lacey whispered.

Sara released her, and then she was taken into Oliver's arms.

"I'm so sorry, Lacey."

The tears came quickly, but she gulped them away. With a strained voice, she said, "Come in, guys."

Sara was Lacey's next-door neighbor and childhood friend. Their childhood play dates and sleepovers bonded them for life and there was no one else Lacey can think of who knew her as well as Sara did; except maybe Oliver, Sara's boyfriend of three years and practically a brother to Lacey.

Not only were Sara and Oliver Lacey's best friends, they also just made sense as a couple. They were shy and bookish, fiercely loyal to not only each other, but to Lacey as well, and so in love that she had no doubt that they would end up married one day. Sara was short and nymph-like, with sparkling hazel eyes and chestnut brown hair reaching her shoulders. Oliver was tall and slender, with almond shaped dark brown eyes, olive skin, and jet-black curls atop his head.

Lacey led her friends into the living room and gestured towards the black leather couch.

"Hi, kids," William said as he walked into the room.

"Hello, Mr. Windham." Sara stood up

and nodded respectfully.

"I hope you're well." Said Oliver, then winced, hoping that his comment wasn't insensitive.

William nodded and smiled assuredly. "All things considered, thank God." He seemed alone, like he didn't want to leave them.

They made small talk about school and work; all the while Lacey and Sara shared a look. Sara narrowed her eyebrows, feeling as if her friend had something to tell her.

Lacey wanted to talk to her friends alone and luckily, her father didn't sit with them long.

"I'll leave you guys to talk, then." William got up with a creak of the chair and left them alone.

"There's something else." Lacey whispered. She leaned forward and beckoned them to do so as well. "After we came home yesterday, my dad dropped a bomb on me."

Sara tilted her head while Oliver became wide-eyed.

"He told me I'm adopted."

Sara gasped.

Lacey nodded. "Yes and not just that. Apparently, I wasn't alone when they found me in the park."

"Wait, wait, and backtrack." Oliver shook his head in confusion.

With a deep breath, Lacey continued. "Right, sorry." She began to detail what her father told her the previous day. As she told them the story, she marveled at how easily the words came, as if they didn't affect her at all. In truth, she was just in shock over learning that everything she had ever known about herself had been wrong. Who just leaves a baby on the beach? She wasn't sure if she wanted to find the people who left her to just die.

When she was finished, there was a long silence. She took the moment to tell her friends about the second part. "That isn't all."

Both Sara and Oliver were speechless at the news.

Lacey continued, "He also gave me this book of languages and an antique necklace. Apparently, whoever left me there in that basket also left these items." She motioned for her friends to follow her upstairs.

They reached her room, both of them still speechless.

Lacey immediately went over to her closet and took out the items she had stashed earlier. She gently handed the book to them, along with the lumpy bundle of crepe paper that contained the necklace. She told them about what her father said, about the possibly cursed necklace.

"Wow," Sara whispered as she leafed through the thick volume, "I've never seen a book like this before. It looks ancient."

Lacey nodded. "And the weird thing is that my dad can't decipher the language."

Oliver and Sara looked up with identical wide gazes.

"Your dad?" Oliver echoed. "Then it must be some alien language. I have never known your father not be able to identify a language."

Lacey hung her head.

Sara laid a hand on Oliver's arm, subtly quieting him. "What are we going to do, Lacey?"

Suddenly, warmth spread through Lacey's entire body. She looked up and gave Sara a grateful smile. Sara's immediate response was to help Lacey with whatever she decided, and for that, Lacey was forever thankful.

"Well, I suppose I should find my birth parents," She shrugged, still unsure if she should. Maybe they abandoned her for a reason. The book and necklace were surely from them, and in order to figure them out, she had to find her parents. "But where would I even look?"

Sara leaned forward and took Lacey's hand. "WE will look." She held the book up. "This is a clue to who they could be."

"How?"

"Well, we just find someone who can read it."

"Take the book to people? I don't know…" Lacey trailed off and looked at Oliver's frowning face. His expression was hardly promising.

Sara shook her head. "We can copy a page and take it to the library." She looked at

Oliver hopefully. "It's a start, right?"

Oliver took a deep breath and looked between the two girls. "I don't know, guys."

Lacey tilted her head questioningly.

He clicked his tongue. "Look, Lacey, with the best intentions, I say we just leave it alone. Why go after something when your life is fine?"

"Oliver!" Sara chastised.

"What? I don't think Lacey needs any additional stress right now. Her mom just died!"

Sara bit her lip and looked back at Lacey, who merely shrugged in response. "As much as I want to find out what this is all about, I think Oliver is right. It's not the right time now." In truth, she wasn't even sure if she wanted to find her birth parents. 'What if they were horrible people?'

Sara released a deep breath. "Of course, Lacey," She squeezed her hand and smiled. "I'm here for whatever you need."

"Me too," Oliver added.

As Lacey closed the door behind her friends, William walked up to her.

"You've got some nice friends."

Lacey nodded. "I'm lucky to have them," she murmured.

"What will you do about what I told you, Lacey?"

She chewed on her lower lip. She wasn't entirely sure herself and hated the feeling of not knowing.

William motioned for her to sit down on the living room sofa and followed her.

Lacey sighed. "I think I'm going to wait before doing anything. To be honest, it hasn't sunk in yet, you know?"

William nodded. "That she's gone?" he whispered.

"No. Well, a little. But I was talking about myself. How can I know who I am now?" She stopped, letting the tears flow down her cheeks. They had been held in too long, and now flowed down her face in torrents.

William immediately took her in his arms and held her tightly. "Whatever you decide, Lacey, I'm by your side. I will always be your dad, I promise."

"I love you, Dad."

CHAPTER TWO

Two weeks went by in much of the same manner. A few times, she went inside her room, closed the door, and pulled out the book to once again decipher it on her own. But there was nothing she could understand. Would it remain a mystery forever? If her dad couldn't make sense of the familiar letters in unfamiliar words through all of these years, how could she? Maybe there was no significance to it, and she was merely driving herself insane for no reason. But then, why did someone leave the book and necklace with her as a baby? There had to be some sort of importance.

She stood in front of the bus stop, ready for the normalcy of school. Her knuckles nearly turned white as she squeezed the straps of her red Puma backpack. She wore jeans and a black long-sleeved t-shirt, and had her hair pulled back in a low ponytail.

Suddenly, the back of her neck prickled with the feeling of being watched and she whipped her head around. Finding no one, she turned back, slightly embarrassed. Her heart thudded against her chest and she took a few deep breaths to calm herself. A dread she could not understand claimed her body and she tensed, on edge from the foreign feeling.

Once again, she turned around to find someone staring at her a few feet away. He stood shrouded in a dark hoodie and black pants, and turned away as soon as she looked, disappearing within the gathering crowd of students.

Lacey shook her head, turning her attention to the bus that was pulling up to the stop. Her feet thumped on the metal steps as the driver said hello. She mumbled a quick greeting and found an empty seat near the back. She was now nervous for a different reason entirely. What would it be like to go back to school when everything inside her had changed?

***

Students bustled through the door of the Business building, seemingly going everywhere and nowhere at all. Lacey made her way to the lecture hall for her Business 101 class, the faces around her blurred and unfamiliar. She was making her way over to the steps that lead her to the topmost row when she stopped, hearing a voice calling her name.

She turned to face her classmate Fatima, a girl wearing a light pink scarf around her head that contrasted beautifully with her chocolate-colored skin.

Fatima walked over and gave Lacey a

tight hug. She held Lacey at arm's length, her eyes misty and her mouth downturned into a frown. "How are you doing?" She whispered.

"Fine," Lacey mumbled, looking around at the other students milling into the lecture hall. She had learned to answer that question this way, and it never failed in stopping the other person from asking any more questions.

Fatima, sensing Lacey's discomfort, took her arm and gently guided her up the stairs. They sat on the nearly empty top row. From there they would be able to converse without being overheard.

The hall filled up and the professor arrived. Soon Fatima was immersed in the lecture. Lacey, however, barely listened as the professor droned on and on about business ethics and some reading they were supposed to do before class.

Instead, Lacey's attention diverted to someone staring at her from across the row. She turned her head slowly to face the person in the hoodie and dark jeans, the one who had been at the bus stop that morning. She could now see his face; sallow skin and blank eyes that looked away as soon as she caught him staring.

Lacey nudged Fatima's arm, then pointed to the guy in the hoodie. "Who's that?" She whispered.

Fatima turned to look and then shrugged.

"I've never seen him before," Lacey mused, "and he doesn't seem like he's a student here."

Fatima looked at the guy again. "I don't know, Lacey. It's a pretty big class." She drew her attention back to her laptop to take notes.

Lacey bit her lower lip. Something about the guy made her uneasy; perhaps it was the way he was just staring at her, but it was also something else. He didn't have a backpack or any books. He barely seemed to be paying attention to the lecture, as if he has just walked into the wrong class. However, when class ended, he was gone before Lacey could get a chance to confront him.

During lunch, she saw him again.

She sat across from Fatima with a shared tray of fries between them. She picked at the salad on her tray, put off by the sad, wilting lettuce.

"I'm going to organize a rally in the south courtyard next week." Fatima was a very active member of the university student union and she organized a rally nearly every week. But, for the life of her, Lacey could not pay attention to whatever it was Fatima was rallying about this time. Probably 'save the orcas' or something. She couldn't keep up anymore.

Lacey tuned out Fatima and brushed a strand of hair behind her ear. Her eyes floated up and she caught someone staring at her.

This time, he was seated two tables over and no longer wearing his hoodie. He had a mop of unruly dirty blond hair and eyes that pierced the distance between them. This time, he didn't look away when Lacey caught him staring. Her heart beat loudly at the sheer anger in his gaze and she was the one to look away now.

She stood up abruptly, nearly knocking down her chair.

"What's wrong?!" Fatima's almond-shaped brown eyes widened.

Lacey shook her head. "I-uh, need to go home. Dad's alone."

Fatima nodded. "Is everything okay?"

Lacey attempted to smile and then gulped. "Yes. I'll see you tomorrow, okay?"

Before Fatima could respond, Lacey picked up her tray of uneaten food, dumped it in the nearest trashcan, and zoomed out of the cafeteria.

***

On the bus home, Lacey clutched her bag to her chest and kept her gaze on her feet. Maybe she wasn't ready to face the normalcy of school, after all. Even as she told herself this, she knew that it wasn't true. The guy in the hoodie was just put her off. His constant staring was unexpected and intimidating. What did he want?

Unbeknownst to Lacey, the object of her fear sat not far from her. Though he faced the side, he kept sending quick looks at her. He noticed her dark hair covering her face, the grief in her body language. Momentarily, he felt a pang of pity for the girl, but he shook it away. There was a reason he was following her, and he couldn't rest until he found what he had been ordered to find.

When the bus stopped, he waited for her to walk off before bouncing off his seat and following her.

He lost her in the crowd for a few moments and whipped his head to and fro. There! She stood a few paces away from, still as a rock. She began to turn around and he immediately jumped behind a tree. A peek is all it took to see that she had begun walking.

The street was lined with townhouses with jutting balconies that served no purpose in Toronto's usually cold weather. Why people chose to live here was beyond him, but how could he understand when he came from a place that was always in opposition to this? He had not known anything else until now.

He watched as Lacey stopped near a house with a set of stairs leading up to the front door; it was one of the few that had baskets of flowers hanging atop the porch. Thick vases lined the brick walkway, adorned with colorful plants that seemed to be wilting. Lacey took out a shiny key from the pocket of her bag and disappeared inside of the house.

A smile overtook him automatically as

he watched the house for a few minutes. On the second floor was a window, through which he could see Lacey pull the blinds down. He noted the number in front of the house and walked away down the street. The human language was foreign to him, but he had learned enough for this mission.

Long, slim fingers reached for something in the pocket of his jeans and he pulled out a square cell phone the size of his palm. He pressed a button and the screen jumped to life, flashing in a kaleidoscope of colors. He tapped it a few times, and then spoke into it. His voice was deep and strong, with no sense of hesitation. "I have found the location."

"Good." A silky voice glided out of the phone and across the air like a snake. "Have my items been spotted?"

"Not at the moment." He replied.

"Update when successful." The voice did not sound angry, but he could never be sure.

"I will."

"I am relying on you. Do not disappoint me. I have been betrayed most heavily."

He frowned in sudden sympathy. "I will find your stolen objects." He said more vehemently than he first attempted to.

The voice laughed. "Good boy."

The screen shut off as the call ended. He stashed the device in his pocket once again and continued walking away from Lacey's house. He'd volunteered for this mission and he would do anything he could to succeed. Justice would prevail, he would see to that personally.

***

Lacey awoke from the dream trickling away like it always did. There was a face... her mind attempted to remember any defining features, but the image left her mind as quickly as she tried to piece it together.

With a huff, she pulled herself out of bed and got ready for the day. Before she left, she snuck a quick look at the bundle that contained the book and necklace. Today, however, she didn't have the luxury of time to take it out and go over it. She would go through it another day.

The day at school was like any other before… she shook her head. It was a seemingly normal day, as if her life hasn't turned upside down in the last month. She went to her Criminology class and was able to concentrate more than she was able to the day before. Fatima didn't have class today and Lacey was slightly grateful. She didn't think she could deal with her rants today.

On the bus home was when she spotted him. A smirk automatically overtook her lips at the sight. He was not wearing his hoodie today, and his dirty blond curls were somewhat less messy. He was doing a poor job of trying to be inconspicuous.

Suddenly, as he began to turn his head toward Lacey, she immediately looked down at the book in her hands, as if she was unaware of his presence. She flipped a page with a broken, bitten nail, under the pretense that she was reading. She could feel his gaze upon her and it took all of her power not to look up at him.

When the bus rolled to a stop, she placed her book in her backpack and swiftly exited with the crowd. The musky smell of too many people enveloped her and she held her breath momentarily. If he wasn't following her, she would turn around to find the street empty. She released a breath. He could simply have been another student at the university, one that took the same bus as her. Why was she so intimidated by his presence? She knew the reason; it was his staring at her with that look.

When the crowd passed, she was not surprised to find him standing in front of the empty road, staring at her.

His dark eyes widened and he began to look away. But before he could take a step away, she marched up to him.

"Hey!"

He stopped in his tracks and turned to look at her.

She nearly gasped at the look on his face.

His lips were twisted into a scowl and his eyes were narrowed into slits of anger? Hatred? She tried to register the unfamiliar face, trying her hardest to find some sort of familiarity. Upon finding none, she gulped down her shock, and took a step closer. "Are you following me?" Her voice was surprisingly stronger than she felt.

He glared at her before finally speaking

in a deep baritone.

"Yes."

CHAPTER THREE

Lacey immediately took a step back from him, wanting desperately for a gaping hole to open up and swallow her whole. The glint in his eyes was angry, even dangerous.

She managed to choke out, "Why?"

Just as suddenly as it appeared, the angry glint from his expression disappeared, replaced by a sincere smile. "Sorry, I didn't mean to freak you out."

'Well, you did,' she wanted to say. She took a breath instead. Maybe she was on edge more than she normally would be. He wouldn't be standing talking to her if he wanted to hurt her, right? She raised an eyebrow expectantly.

"I live just a block over," he pointed down the street, where it turned into the next one, "I'm renting a room with the sweetest old lady." He laughed a little forcedly.

Lacey did not respond.

He scratched the back of his head. "I'm Matt. I just started at U of T, and um, heard about your mom. I've been trying to work up the courage to speak to you, but I didn't know how…" He looked away as he trailed off, a faraway look in his dark brown eyes.

Lacey wished to say something to this stranger, but her mind mulled over the information he gave her. She thought she believed him but doesn't know what he wanted from her.

"I'm really sorry about your mom. It must be very difficult to lose her."

This time, Lacey looked away, tears prickling at her eyes. Simple words could not describe the loss. She nearly turned away, but politeness rooted her to the spot. "Thank you," she murmured.

Another smile lit up Matt's face, and this time Lacey could see that he was not as intimidating as he first looked. In fact, he just looked like a regular person.

Lacey gave him a small smile in return.

Encouraged by the gesture, Matt continued, "I just lost a parent too. I was also hoping that we could, maybe, get to know each other a bit?"

Lacey thought the suggestion was a bit blunt, but shrugged and agreed.

He took a breath, seemingly of relief. "Oh, great. It'll be good to not have to ride the bus and sit in classes alone."

Her smile widened. She could

understand that sentiment completely. "Just make sure you don't just stare at anyone from a distance, and you won't have trouble meeting new people."

To her relief, he laughed instead of being offended.

"Guess social interactions aren't my strong suit."

Someone who can laugh at himself, be it a forced laugh How refreshing. Lacey needed more people like that in her life, especially now. She was then suddenly aware of how his brown eyes sparkled when he laughed, crinkling at the corners. She was suddenly aware of the deep musky scent of his cologne and the flattering button-down shirt he wore with dark-washed jeans. She felt her cheeks flush at the proximity that suddenly seemed very close. She cleared her throat. "I should get going."

Matt nodded. "Me too, the old lady gets lonely."

Lacey laughed her first laugh after what seemed like ages.

**

"Have you given any thought to what the language in the book could be, Lacey?" William asked over his plate of spaghetti.

The question wasn't completely out of the blue. Lacey knew that he has been thinking of what her next steps would be. In truth, she had not thought of finding her birth parents recently. She wanted to, of course, but the task seemed daunting at best and impossible at worst.

She shrugged, "I don't know."

His eyes narrowed for a fraction of a second before he masked it by taking a bite. Then he nodded in understanding.

Lacey gave him the tiniest of smiles. Was he worried that she would leave him once she found her birth parents? Would she? Who knew where they were? And where would she even start looking for them?

They continued eating their meal in silence, and after she bid her father goodbye and walked up to her bedroom.

There, she went inside the closet and pulled out the package with the book and necklace. She removed the paper wrapping from around the book and heaved it onto her lap. It was quite impressive, with leather binding and engraved words on the cover. There was a symbol atop the words and she inspected it closely as she hadn't before. It was a crest with a roaring lion surrounded by vines. Beneath the lion were a grassy field and a sun that seemed to be spreading its rays through the entire crest.

She opened the cover to find old, yellowing pages that smell of parchment and dust. She leafed aimlessly through the book for a while, attempting unsuccessfully to read the words. Careful hands flipped the pages without her thinking, until she came across the end of the book.

The back cover was thicker than the front, and when she pulled at the edge, it seemed as if it was padded by something inside. She carefully inserted a finger into the flap and her skin touched a piece of paper. With slow movements, she removed the paper and held it up to her face.

Her heart skipped a beat. The letter was written in loopy cursive, in English! Without hesitation, her eyes trailed over it.

Dearest child,

Stay safe. Stay alive. Be careful of Val. Keep this *grimoire* close and keep our family *riviere* closer. It is far more valuable than it appears. Don't let them take it from you. We will always love you, our princess.

-Willow and Rami

Lacey read, then reread the letter. She

turned the page over to find the same crest as the one on the cover of the book. Instead of answering questions, the letter brought more. Family riviere? She didn't know what that meant. But then, there was something else that came with the book. She carefully shoved the letter back inside the flap in the back cover, the turned to the lumpy package that contained the necklace. Could this be what Willow and Rami meant by the riviere?

She hastily opened the package. The stones sparkled in the dusk light that filtered in through her window. It clinked slightly as she picked it up and she slowly turned it around to find the same crest engraved on the gold behind the biggest stone.

What could it mean? Before she was able to dwell on the question, the doorbell rang. Lacey quickly wrapped the objects and shoved them back into her closet.

Her father thudded over to the door and opened it.

"Hello, Mr. Windham." Sara's cheery voice said.

Lacey stood up and brushed herself off. She needed to tell someone of what she just found, or else she would burst. She rushed down the stairs, and without so much as a word of hello, pulled Sara by the arm all the way up to her room.

"Thank you, Mr. Windham!" Sara called from the top of the stairs before Lacey closed her bedroom door.

Lacey took a deep breath, and then turned to a frowning Sara.

"I've just found something," Lacey explained. She took out the book and necklace.

Sara's large green eyes became even wider as she reached for the book. "Did you find out something about the book?"

Lacey nodded. "Not just this." She opened the back cover, took out the letter from the flap, and handed it toward her friend.

Sara hesitantly reached for it, then opened it and read it. She looked up at Lacey, her mouth silently open. "What does it mean?" she finally choked out.

Lacey showed Sara the crest on the necklace and the back of the letter. "Have you ever seen this crest before?"

Sara ran her fingers over the engraved crest on the back of the necklace, then the cover of the book. She shook her head. "The letter called the book a grimoire."

"What does that mean?"

"A grimoire is a book of spells…" Sara trailed off, watching the book carefully.

Something inside Lacey's mind clicked. "My dad told me that when my mom put on the necklace, things around her started happening. He said that it might be cursed." Lacey had never been the superstitious type, but even she could not deny that the existence of the book of spells made it seem more believable.

Sara gasped. She, on the other hand, did believe openly in the occult. She was suddenly afraid and uncomfortable in the presence of the objects and wanted nothing to do with them. "Put them away, Lacey," she warned, "maybe it's for the best if we don't find out what it means."

Lacey chewed her lip, disheartened by her friend's rejection. Sara had always been careful about things, wanting to stay in her comfort zone. She barely ever talked to new people in school or goes to any events that were different than what she has always done.

Lacey agreed to put the objects away, but she knew that she was one step closer to finding her birth parents. And this wasn't the time to give up.

They were jolted into movement by another ring of the doorbell. Lacey looked at

Sara. "Oliver?"

Sara shook her head. "He's tutoring tonight."

Lacey put the objects back where they were, stuffing the letter in the middle of the book, and shuffled Sara downstairs.

At the front door stood Matt, speaking politely with her father.

William turned when he saw Lacey approach.

"This is Matt. He's new at U of T." She explained.

William nodded and swiftly left them all alone.

"I was wondering if you're free tonight." Matt said to Lacey before his gaze travelled over to Sara. "But if you're busy…"

"Nope!" Sara interjected, sending Lacey

a meaningful glance before she stepped forward.

Lacey resisted the urge to roll her eyes. She was sure that Sara had something else in her mind, but Matt was just someone who lived close to her and went to her school. She couldn't even call him a friend yet.

"Well, we were just talking about seeing a movie. Why don't you join us, Matt?" Sara asked with a giggle.

Lacey glared at her friend, who barely notices. They had certainly not been making plans to go anywhere.

Matt looked at Lacey for some kind of approval, and then turned back to Sara. "Okay, sure, thanks." He smiled, unsure.

Sara looked between the two and her lips curled into a smile that is not at all subtle.

Lacey wished to pull her friend away and scold her, but she was already walking out of the house and asking Matt questions about where he moved from. Lacey couldn't help but follow along and seethed at the fact that Sara's mind was no doubt running a mile a minute.

***

The line in front of the movie theater was filled with loud high school kids enjoying their Friday night, but Lacey felt like anything but fun. Her mind still buzzed with the information she learned about the grimoire and wanted to go through it again to find out if she could understand something. Maybe she could ask someone online and they could decipher it for her. Maybe the reason her dad was never able to read the words was that he never took it seriously as a book of spells.

"Lacey?" Matt waved a hand in front of her face. "Are you okay?"

She nodded absentmindedly and followed the two towards the theater.

The movie was Sara's choice: a romcom

filled with sappy characters and a predictable plot. Lacey barely paid attention.

Lacey could feel that Matt's attention was trained on her through the entire movie. He wished for a chance to have Lacey alone so he could casually ask about the stolen objects. Val was very concise in her instructions find the grimoire and necklace and bring them to the location; then, and only then, would she send him back home.

Luckily, a chance presented itself after the movie. As patrons trickled out of the theater, he turned to the two girls, clutching his stomach.

"Let's get some dinner."

Lacey shrugged and looked at Sara.

Sara smiled. "Sure." She led them out of the theater and towards a restaurant nearby.

The late November night was chilly, with a breeze that cut through his skin and whistled through his hair. He hurried after the girls toward the *Boston Pizza*.

Sara turned around at the door. "Actually, guys, I just remembered that I have to get home."

Before Lacey could so much get a word in, Sara left the two with a wave and a swift word of goodbye.

Matt turned to Lacey and smiled. "Guess it's just us, then."

"I guess," Lacey mumbled, slightly anxious over the two of them together, alone.

Matt internally celebrated. If he could get her to open up, he would have a chance to ask her questions. He opened the door to the restaurant and they stepped inside.

Chatter filled the place, with the mingling scent of different foods. It was much warmer inside and Matt was immediately at ease. A look toward Lacey revealed that she was much more relaxed than she was outside.

They were seated at a little booth in the back of the restaurant, away from the crowd. Lacey picked up her menu and disappeared behind it. Matt barely read his, not caring what he ended up getting. Instead, he mulled over how he would bring up the topic of her parents. More importantly, *how am I supposed to get her to open up?*

When the waiter left with their orders, Matt leaned across the table to fix her with an intense gaze. "It must be really hard without your mom, Lacey."

She startled, taken aback by his blunt statement. "Uh-yeah," she stammered, "but I still have my dad." She looked away, to a family with young kids gibbering on to their laughing parents. She returned her glance to Matt to find that he was staring at her intensely.

"I'm sorry," he said, "I didn't mean to make you feel uncomfortable." His brown eyes had sincerity to them and something else too. Something he was keeping hidden. His gaze was searching, as if he was aware of something Lacey wasn't privy to. She looked down at her limp hands on the table.

Matt cleared his throat. "I-I also lost my family." He whispered.

Lacey suddenly looked at him, her eyebrows narrowed in sympathy.

Encouraged, he continued. "My parents died when I was little, so I don't really remember them. But they did leave a few things behind." He smiled. "Heirlooms, I guess you could say."

Lacey suddenly perked up, but before she had a chance to speak, the food arrived. After the waiter left, she looked over her plate of pasta to catch the same intense look on Matt's face as before. Neither of them touched their food.

"What kind of heirlooms?" Lacey asked.

Matt didn't hesitate to speak up, "Just some books and an old necklace that belonged to my great-grandmother." He looked away with a wistful glint in his eyes. "It was the most beautiful thing, with diamonds and emeralds. I've never seen anything else like it."

Lacey put a hand on her mouth, covering the gasp that left her lips with a cough; an antique necklace? She thought briefly, 'an odd coincidence, or did he know something. Something he kept to himself.' She couldn't forget that first look.

"Unfortunately, the necklace was stolen many years ago."

Lacey could not breathe. Did her birth parents steal the necklace? Perhaps that was the reason it was so valuable.

Matt asked, "Do you have any family heirlooms?"

At the time, Lacey did not find the question strange. She shook her head. "I don't know anything about my family, actually." She managed to choke out. She wasn't sure that she could trust his words.

Lacey was suddenly not hungry and wanted nothing more than to leave the restaurant. She opened her bag and took out a twenty-dollar bill. She slapped it down on the table and abruptly stood up. "I just remembered that I have some homework left." Without waiting for a reply, she left Matt sitting there open-mouthed.

Once home, she rushed upstairs to her closet. Once again, she read the letter and her heart sank.

'Willow and Rami, what is this all about?' She cried to herself.

CHAPTER FOUR

There was a thud on the porch outside. Startled, Lacey scrambled to hide the items back in her closet, laying the letter on top of the pile in her haste. She stood up quickly and rushed to her bedroom door.

"Dad?" She called out.

There was no answer and she went downstairs. Finding the kitchen and living room empty, she checked the garage. The car was gone, meaning her father must have gone out somewhere.

Something wasn't right. She took a deep

breath, trying to calm her nerves, but it didn't help much. Suddenly her stomach rumbled, startling her with the loud noise. She realized what it was and remembered the huge bowl of pasta she had left untouched at Boston Pizza. Embarrassed, she breathed a laugh, shook her head and headed back to the kitchen.

She stared into the fridge for what seemed a very long time before deciding on a day-old rotisserie chicken, some mayo and a loaf of bread. When she closed the fridge she nearly dropped all of it when she saw the young man standing there, staring at her with narrowed, dark brown eyes.

"Matt!" she exclaimed, clutching the bread to her chest. "You scared me! How did you get in here?"

"You left the front door open." His tone was relaxed, but his smirk was cold.

Lacey smiled, but she didn't mean it. Even though she had rushed inside, she knew she had locked that door. However, she tried to answer flippantly. "Ah well, my mistake. Thanks for letting me know. I was just going to bed, so…"

Matt's smirk widened, as he gestured toward the half chicken. "That doesn't look like a pillow, now does it?"

Her brow furrowed. Was he just being rude? No, there was something more, something sinister about him. Casually, she laid the food items on the counter. "I was going to make a sandwich and carry it to my room to eat before bed, as if it's any of your business."

"Let's stop pretending now."

She tilted her head and chewed on her lip. "I don't know what you're talking about."

"Yes, you do." He took a small step forward, and Lacey was grateful that the kitchen counter still stood between them. "You know where my family's necklace is, don't you?"

Her eyes widened. How does he know? How much danger was she in? "Why would I know anything about that, Matt? You're not making sense."

"You have them. I know they are in this house somewhere. Don't lie to me." He leaned in, placing his hands on the counter and flexing the muscles in his arms.

"I think you need to leave." Lacey regretted the tremble in her voice as she said it.

"Just give me the grimoire and the necklace, and you won't see me again."

They stared at each other for a long time, wondering who would break the stalemate. Then Lacey grabbed the jar of mayo, threw it at Matt's face, and ran.

She heard Matt's grunt of surprise and heard the jar smash on the floor a second later, but she was already racing down the hallway. Luckily, he followed her instead of searching upstairs. Reaching the garage, she leaped over the small steps leading to ground level and scrambled to the side door. She would run into the street and scream until all the neighbors came out of their houses.

But when she flung the door open, a woman stood there, tall and straight, with ink black hair, piercing green eyes and a smile like a serpent. "Where do you think you're going?" Her voice slithered through her teeth and she stepped in through the door, forcing Lacey to retreat a few steps.

Just then, Matt reached the garage. His nose was bloody and his jeans were still covered in blobs of mayo from when the jar exploded on the floor. He skidded to a halt when he saw the woman and his confidence drained away. "Val. What are you "

"You were taking too long!" the woman barked. "Now find the grimoire and the riviere and bring them to me!"

Val? Was this the Val mentioned in the letter? Be careful of Val, it had warned. The letter also said to protect the book and the necklace and she was about to fail that task.

"What do you want from me?" Lacey curled her hands into fists to stop them shaking. "Get out of my house!"

"All in good time, little girl," she growled. "Give me what I want and it will all be over."

That didn't sound hopeful, Lacey thought. Whoever Val was, she was dangerous, just like the letter said. She wanted to save her parents' belongings as they had asked, but Lacey wondered if she would even make it through this night alive. She fervently hoped something would happen to change the odds.

Matt appeared at the top of the steps. Val snapped, "Hurry up, boy; bring the book to me!" However, he did not move. Lacey saw that he was reading the letter from her parents, a look of confusion on his face. Then he turned the page over and saw the emblem on the back. He gasped.

"Lacey? *You* are the lost princess?" He stared at her as if seeing her for the first time.

"Right now, Matt!" Val ordered. "Don't keep me waiting any longer."

Then Lacey saw it. A blob of the mayo had dripped onto the floor just below the steps. And Matt's foot was right above it. She tensed in readiness.

Had he been hurrying to obey Val's orders, he might have stepped wide and missed it. But Matt was still staring dazedly at Lacey when he slowly stepped down. His foot slid on the oily mess, and he flailed helplessly as his body hit the stairs.

Val and Lacey lunged for the items he dropped. Val grabbed the grimoire, and Lacey got the riviere. Automatically, she slipped it over her head to keep her hands free.

Something changed.

Lacey could suddenly feel her body

filling with a new energy. The jewels in the necklace began to glow, as if they also felt this new energy. She turned to Matt, who was staring at her open-mouthed.

"Stupid boy! Get it back!" Val screamed.

After a quick, confused glance at Val, Matt turned and reached toward Lacey, speaking quickly. "Lacey! Whatever you do, don "

Lacey raised a hand to fend him off and a shockwave of power sent Matt sprawling back on the stairs. He groaned.

Val sneered in disgust at Lacey and opened the grimoire, quickly locating a page. With a finger pointed toward Lacey, she began to read, the words at once familiar and unfamiliar to Lacey's ears.

The riviere around Lacey's neck began to burn, she cried out, reaching for it.

"No!" Matt shouted. "Don't take it off!"

He launched himself at Val, stopping her flow of words. As the two fell, Val kicked out and caught Lacey's leg, and all three crashed to the floor.

Val managed to grab Lacey's ankle in a vicelike grip. Lacey tried to kick the hand away, but it was no use. Matt also grabbed her hand, and the three struggled for dominance. Lacey, exhausted and scared, closed her eyes and wished for her father.

Suddenly, she was surrounded by darkness. The garage, the house, Toronto, everything was gone and the struggling trio were falling through a black void. Lacey felt Val's grip loosen and the sensation of her hand fell away. Matt's fingers grasped for hers a second longer, but then they too were gone. The void seemed to go on endlessly.

Then Lacey blinked.

She was lying on the ground. She lay there for several moments, relieved that the sense of falling had finally stopped. The darkness wasn't as dark either; a few flecks of light danced slowly above her.

When she felt a little calmer, she sat up and looked around. There was no sign of Val or Matt, which was good. But then, there was no sign of anyone or anything she knew. She was sitting in a grove of trees and the twilight-dim sky peeked through the leaves. She looked down at her legs and saw she was wearing the same clothes at least. With a gasp, she reached for her neck and then exhaled gratefully when she felt the necklace still around her throat.

What was that power she felt from the necklace? How did she escape Val and Matt? Are they somewhere in this place too, or did they disappear into the void? Where was she, anyway? So many confusing and frightening questions flew through Lace's mind. One thought kept returning, the scariest thought of all.

How in the world was she going to get home?

The next book in this series:

Riviere and the Stone Cup

Book 2

Book and Necklace

Review This Book

P.S. It means the world to me that you brought my book. Writing is my passion and I look forward to YOUR feedback.

So if you liked this book, I'd like to ask for a small favor. Would you be so kind to leave a review on Amazon? It'd be very much appreciated!

From your friend,

Taylor Wilson

Printed in Great Britain
by Amazon

69333251R00051